LET'S LOOK AT BODY SYSTEMS!

IKER'S INCREDIBLE IMMUNE SYSTEM

by Mari Schuh
illustrated by Ed Myer

GRASSHOPPER

Tools for Parents & Teachers

Grasshopper Books enhance imagination and introduce the earliest readers to fiction with fun storylines and illustrations. The easy-to-read text supports early reading experiences with repetitive sentence patterns and sight words.

Before Reading

- Discuss the cover illustration. What do they see?
- Look at the glossary together. Discuss the words.

Read the Book

- Read the book to the child, or have him or her read independently.
- "Walk" through the book and look at the illustrations. Who is the main character? What is happening in the story?

After Reading

- Prompt the child to think more. Ask: How does your immune system fight germs to keep you healthy? How can you help keep your immune system strong?

Grasshopper Books are published by Jump!
5357 Penn Avenue South
Minneapolis, MN 55419
www.jumplibrary.com

Copyright © 2022 Jump! International copyright reserved in all countries. No part of this book may be reproduced in any form without written permission from the publisher.

Library of Congress Cataloging-in-Publication Data

Names: Schuh, Mari C., 1975- author. | Myer, Ed, illustrator.
Title: Iker's incredible immune system / by Mari Schuh; illustrated by Ed Myer.
Description: Grasshopper books. Minneapolis, MN: Jump!, Inc., [2022]
Series: Let's look at body systems!
Includes index.
Audience: Grades 2-3
Identifiers: LCCN 2021040237 (print)
LCCN 2021040238 (ebook)
ISBN 9781636906416 (hardcover)
ISBN 9781636906423 (paperback)
ISBN 9781636906430 (ebook)
Subjects: LCSH: Immune system–Juvenile literature.
Classification: LCC QR181.8 .S38 2022 (print)
LCC QR181.8 (ebook)
DDC 616.07/9–dc23
LC record available at https://lccn.loc.gov/2021040237
LC ebook record available at https://lccn.loc.gov/2021040238

Editor: Jenna Gleisner
Direction and Layout: Anna Peterson
Illustrator: Ed Myer

Printed in the United States of America at Corporate Graphics in North Mankato, Minnesota.

Table of Contents

Fighting Germs... **4**

Where in the Body?.. **22**

Let's Review!... **23**

To Learn More... **23**

Glossary.. **24**

Index... **24**

Fighting Germs

"My throat is still sore, Grandpa. Will this cold ever go away?" asks Iker.

"Your body needs time to fight the virus," his grandpa answers.

"Virus?" asks Iker. "I thought it was just a cold."

"A cold is caused by a virus," his grandpa says. "A virus is a type of germ. Germs are so tiny you can't see them. But they can sneak into your body, like on dirty hands. They can make you sick. Your immune system helps keep these germs out of your body. It also attacks them if they get in."

germs

Achoo! Iker sneezes. "Why is my nose running so much?" he asks.

"Your body is trying to get rid of the virus," his grandpa answers. "You feel sick because your immune system is working hard to attack the virus."

9

"Where is the immune system in my body?" asks Iker.

"Different cells, tissues, and organs are all part of it," his grandpa says. "It includes your tonsils, spleen, lymph nodes, bone marrow, and white blood cells."

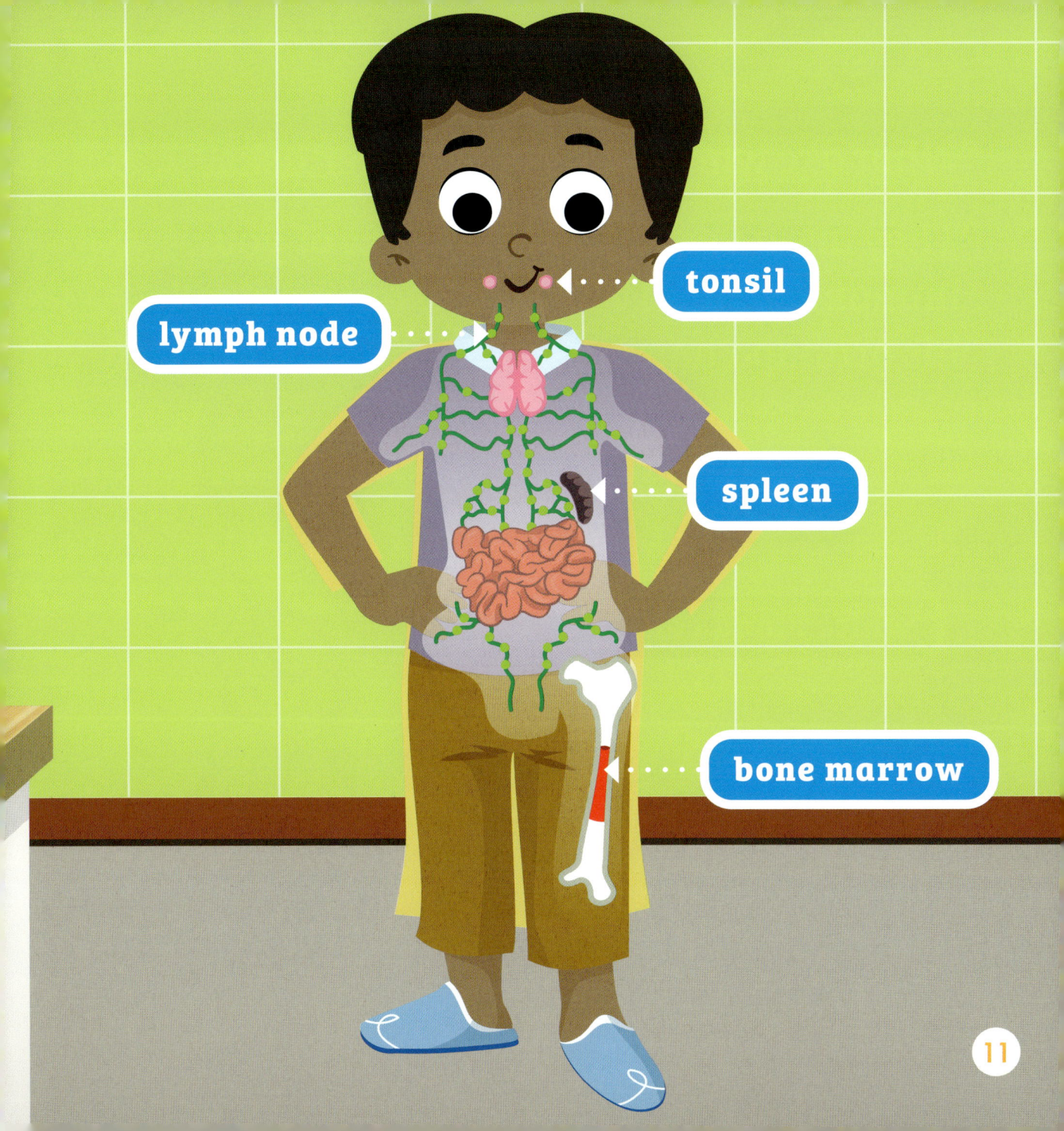

lymph node

tonsil

spleen

bone marrow

"What are white blood cells?" Iker asks.

"They are a very important part of your immune system! They make antibodies," his grandpa answers.

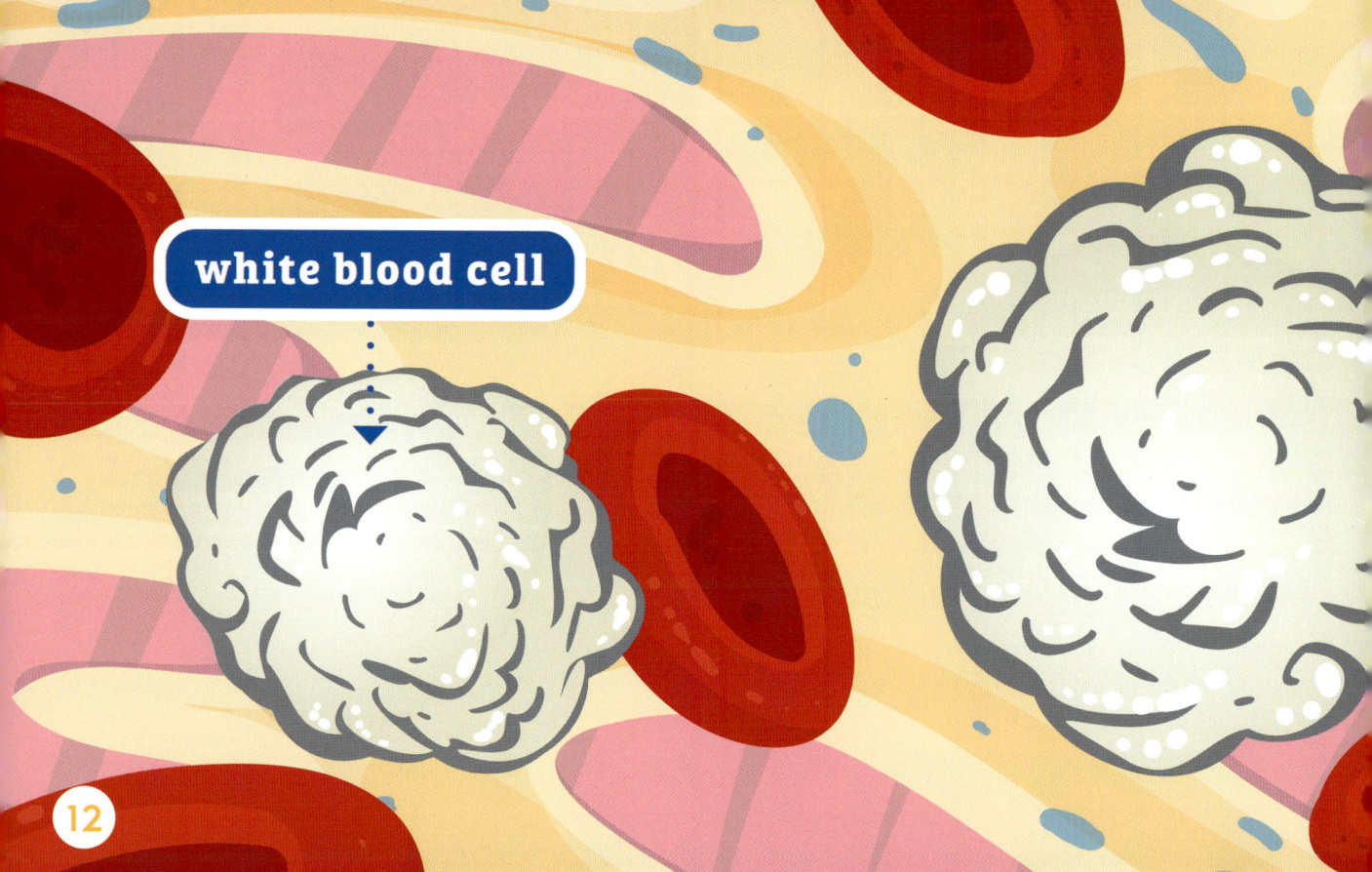

white blood cell

germ

antibody

"Antibodies attach to germs. They can kill them before you get sick," he explains.

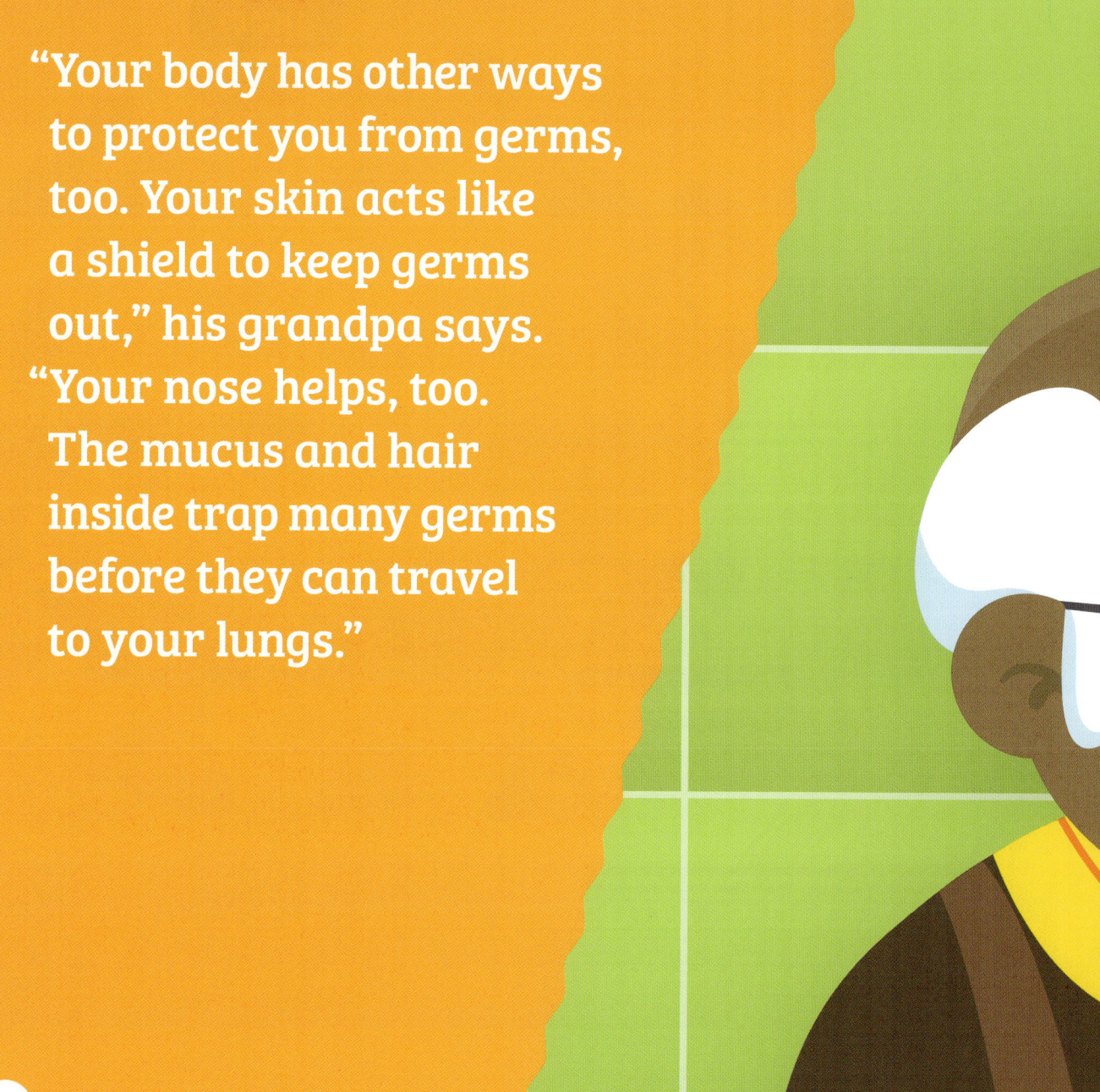

"Your body has other ways to protect you from germs, too. Your skin acts like a shield to keep germs out," his grandpa says. "Your nose helps, too. The mucus and hair inside trap many germs before they can travel to your lungs."

mucus

hair

"Wow! How else does my body fight off germs?" asks Iker.

"Lots of ways! When you breathe air or eat food, your tonsils destroy germs," his grandpa says. "Stomach acid destroys them in your food. Tears in your eyes wash away dust and germs. Sweat helps, too! It pushes away germs and dirt on your skin."

17

"Sometimes your immune system needs a little help," his grandpa says. "Remember when you got a flu shot? Vaccines help protect you from viruses."

"Washing your hands kills germs, too," says his grandpa. "But germs aren't always bad. Being around them teaches your immune system how to fight them."

"It's important to stay active, get enough sleep, and eat healthy foods. These things help keep your immune system strong so it can fight germs," his grandpa says.

"My immune system sounds incredible!" Iker says.

"It is!" his grandpa says. "You'll feel better in no time."

21

Where in the Body?

What body parts make up your immune system? Take a look!

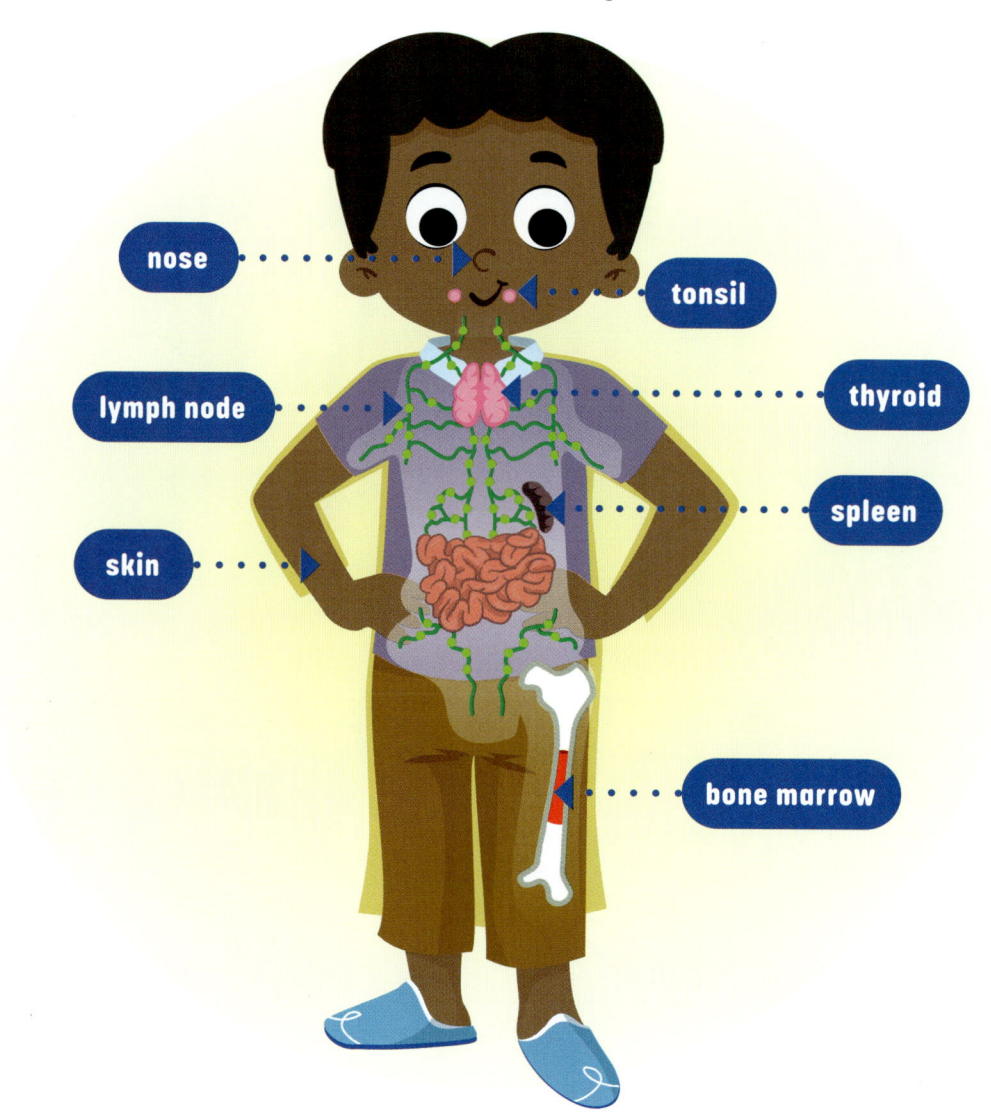

- nose
- tonsil
- lymph node
- thyroid
- spleen
- skin
- bone marrow

Let's Review!

How do you and your immune system help keep germs out of your body?

sneezing

sweating

washing

getting vaccinated

To Learn More

Finding more information is as easy as 1, 2, 3.

1. Go to www.factsurfer.com
2. Enter "**Iker'sincredibleimmunesystem**" into the search box.
3. Choose your book to see a list of websites.

Glossary

antibodies: Proteins produced by the immune system to fight viruses.

cells: The smallest parts of living things. A microscope is needed to see cells.

germ: A microscopic living thing, especially one that causes disease.

mucus: A thick, slimy liquid that coats and protects the inside of your mouth, nose, throat, and other breathing passages.

organs: Parts of the body that do certain jobs.

tissues: Masses of similar cells that form parts of organs.

vaccines: Substances usually given by injection to people or animals to protect against disease.

virus: A tiny organism that can reproduce, grow inside cells, and cause disease.

white blood cells: Colorless blood cells that help protect the body against infection.

Index

antibodies 12, 13
bone marrow 10
breathe 16
cold 4, 6
germ 6, 13, 14, 16, 19, 20
hair 14
lungs 14
lymph nodes 10
mucus 14
nose 8, 14

skin 14, 16
sneezes 8
spleen 10
stomach acid 16
sweat 16
tears 16
tonsils 10, 16
vaccines 18
virus 5, 6, 8, 18
white blood cells 10, 12